good deed rain

Books by Allen Frost

Ohio Trio
Bowl of Water
Another Life
Home Recordings
The Mermaid Translation
The Selected Correspondence of Kenneth Patchen
The Wonderful Stupid Man
Saint Lemonade
Playground
Roosevelt
5 Novels
The Sylvan Moore Show
Town in a Cloud
A Flutter of Birds Passing Through Heaven:
    A Tribute to Robert Sund
At the Edge of America
Lake Erie Submarine
The Book of Ticks
I Can Only Imagine
The Orphanage of Abandoned Teenagers
Different Planet
Go with the Flow: A Tribute to Clyde Sanborn
Homeless Sutra
The Lake Walker
A Hundred Dreams Ago
Almost Animals
The Robotic Age
Kennedy
Fable

FABLE

Fable ©2018
Allen Frost, Good Deed Rain
Bellingham, Washington
ISBN 978-1-64440-083-8

Writing: Allen Frost
Cover Paintings: Laura Vasyutynska
Cover Production: Fred Sodt
Photos: Allen Frost
Apple: TFK!

"Why did you go out into the countryside?
To see a reed shaken by the wind?"

—*The Secret Books of the Egyptian Gnostics*

FABLE

Allen Frost

FABLE

Introduction......9
The Rabbits Parable..17
Coral & The Admiral......33
11 Ohio Days 75

Perhaps, friends, it is time
To take a stand
Against all this senseless hurt

—Kenneth Patchen

INTRODUCTION:

The week before we left for Ohio, I was woken by a strange echo at 3 AM. It sounded like someone jump-roping. I looked outside and couldn't see the source in the gloom...not until I got up and went downstairs and opened the front door. Someone stood out there on the corner, no shirt on, slapping themselves and motioning like a diver about to leap into the street. Once a car went by, shined on him, and I thought he would dive right into the light. Someone driven mad by the moon and the summer night...It couldn't be good to have that happening in our neighborhood, so I called the police. "There's something wrong with him," I warned. While I waited for them, he wandered out of sight. That would have been hard to explain if he vanished altogether, but soon he returned, running down the sidewalk, followed at a distance by two police cars. I watched them for as long as I could, but when they turned right on Donovan, they were hidden by trees. I wondered if I had made a mistake. Maybe he was just some nutty, slap-happy eccentric, but honestly I didn't get that feeling. He wasn't James Stewart in *Harvey*, a little tipsy on moonlight and dandelion. It was 3:30 as I fell back into bed. Then a fire engine hissed beside the curb. Behind it was an ambulance. Another police car arrived too. I almost ran outside, until I realized that I was only wearing orange underwear and a white t-shirt with a clown face on it. How would that look to the police and paramedics? But after I threw on a plaid shirt and pants and ran out, it was too late. With a loud rumble, the entourage pulled away. I did feel bad about what happened, but the neighborhood soon returned to quiet, just the hushing cars on the highway drifting across the backyard. Still, it took me a while to fall asleep. I had to think about what I was part of.

At first I thought that disruption was some midnight maniac chopping down our butterfly bush. The *buddleja* is not a native species and is considered an invasive weed by some. Just last week, when I got home, I found the torn remains of one on the property line with our neighbor. So I wondered if that same fiend was still on the loose, with vigilante justice in mind.

What can you do with those poor souls whose minds have got tangled up like filament? You can't just have someone acting mad on the sidewalks at night, can you? "There's something wrong with him," was right. He needed help. If you tell the authorities, you need to hope they are caring and trained and helpful to those in need.

And yet, when I stood outside, barefoot on the lawn, I felt that mad freedom too. The stars were out. The Big Dipper handle was ready to pour. The moon was a cut crescent with Mercury gleaming. Why not take off your shirt and slap your skin and run back and forth in the glow? I wasn't afraid of the dark or the hour—I had a picket fence around me and a house up the steps and a sleeping family and a wife in bed. But not everybody does.

There's something wrong going on in this country and I can best relate it in fable: the parable of the rabbits, a bedtime story I wrote for our daughter, and the diary of our trip to Ohio.

I don't want this to be a political book. I'm thinking about compassion and hope—how an event beginning with rabbits fits in, the lesson it taught, as Ohio was nearing. I haven't been to Ohio since 2015. That was when I wrote *Lake Erie Submarine* and Obama was our president. Since then, they have elected another, very different president. The result of a fear campaign. What happens if you terrify people into thinking the things they love are in danger? I didn't know what to expect. I can't understand the logic of that vote. I can understand the huge weight of disappointment in the failures of our government. I agree we are in need of a revolution, but not led by backwards thinking. I know that Coral has heard me going on about this every day for years, like one of those crackpot radio voices. I know it was a topic I could be heard talking about even more as we got closer to Ohio. Coral sat on the couch and listened.

Coral and the Admiral is an old story I began for my daughter Rosa when she was seven. I had it scattered throughout many notebooks. As far as my archaeology reveals, I began this adventure in July 2003. At that time, I was upset at the invasions, wars and our then-president. I didn't like the way things were going and I thought I could help with a children's story. It was meant to be just for Rosa and features things she really said back then as a 7 year old. She explained how to write a poem and she said, "I can hear crickets at night, on the other side of the world." But the story remained incomplete, though notes on it continued through 2009. Meanwhile, during that period I wrote a lot of other books: *Lemonade, Rose Petal Lantern, The Next President, Copper Kettle, White Pond, Sun Mountain Grocery, The Mermaid Translation*, as well as 16 poetry chapbooks. No wonder Coral's story got lost for a while! Fifteen summers later, I had only a vague recollection of it, but I knew it would be perfect for this book, as Coral's dream. It was fascinating for me to rediscover, to finish, and to see how it still mirrors our current situation. Our leaders do create an aura about the time we live in. "I'm a very stable genius," our current president keeps assuring us, while acting the opposite.

I know this will all be ancient history soon. But history has a way of repeating in America. I don't even want to give name to a leader who would tell people: "They will be met with fire and fury like the world has never seen. You will suffer consequences the likes of which few throughout history have ever suffered before." White contrails over Ohio—hundreds scratching up the blue sky above Akron, Cincinnati, Cleveland, Toledo, Columbus—the rumble of a thousand deadly airplane engines…Something terrible happened and we've gone back in time; all those American B-17s and B-24s fell out of their flight paths over 1940s Germany and right now they're overhead. Bombs fall on all those cities; all those people are burned into dust. That's where your war words will take us. It got me so upset I had to watch Laurel and Hardy. *The Living Ghost* helped. The world they live in, they persevere. I don't know how they survive, but they do. Then I had coffee with *The Incredible Shrinking Man.* I went with him into the café, where he met Clarice who said, "The best way to begin is to start thinking about the future. For people like you and me, the world can be a wonderful place. You've got to believe that." And after meeting her, he felt better, saying, "That night I got a grip on life again. I went back to work on my book. It absorbed me completely. I was telling the world of my experience, and with the telling it became easier."

We only had two weeks to rediscover Ohio. Like the Shrinking Man, I was open to the experience, to write down what happened. I also knew I would go to Ohio looking for the things I like. The Ray Bradbury nostalgia for those big treed lanes, crickets, and old towns with Civil War squares. They do have old things I like about America that we don't have here. I know there are still a few drive-in theaters there. I'd love to see one of those 1950s movies, like *Monster on Campus*. I want to hear that voice warn across the tops of parked cars, "Man can use his knowledge to destroy all spiritual values and reduce the race to bestiality. Or he can use his knowledge to increase his understanding to a point far beyond anything now imaginable."

As for the rabbits, I don't see that many around now. It's as if a rabbit wind blew through town. They fell out of the air and were scattered everywhere and now they've pretty much disappeared. I did see one in the backyard. It had the look of a biblical prophet, lean and wary. It might have been hobbling with a cane, its brown Moses robes riffling in the wind, holding out a paw, pointing towards the promised land.

Allen Frost
Bellingham, Washington
End of Summer 2018

PART 1:

THE RABBITS PARABLE

I can hear the owl. Its voice carries across the yard, the street, down the stretch of dead end road into the woods, where another owl answers. I know they are hunting. Those small things out in the grass don't even know what's coming. Earlier this spring we saw a bobcat. It stood just on the wild edge of the woods where a neighbor's lawn began and it watched for rabbits. Every time I walk our dog along this stretch, she looks for them too. That's probably the wolf buried deep in her, something she can't control, but I do feel somewhat at fault for the way this story happened.

There have been more rabbits this year than anytime I can remember. I heard that's because the city trapped every coyote in town. I don't know if that's true, but it's not difficult to accept. It's the sort of thing people do to nature. The coyotes were here and now they're gone. Since then, something has slipped out of balance and there are rabbits everywhere. Not just in the fields and brush, I've seen them in the hedge at the bus stop, one lives under a sculpture where I work, and I swear I've noticed them scamper across the floor at the grocery store. They have adopted a sort of fearlessness of us.

I guess I hoped to keep them on a little bit of edge, so they would be aware that they are prey. Sometimes when our dog would get low, looking lean as a lion when she spotted them, I would let her off her leash. You could tell she got such a joy from that chase. I knew she wouldn't be able to catch one—she's 14 and doesn't that mean 98 years old for a person? It's hard to imagine an old woman that age rattling across the grass to catch a rabbit. The rabbits aren't worried either. They chew clover and let her get closer and then, in a burst of sped-up film, they're gone in a flash, safe in the blackberry. By giving her that thrill, I suppose I allowed her to see herself as a heroic hunting dog, like in *Where the Red Fern Grows*. But it wasn't long before I got a phone call at work.

First though, I have to mention that the rabbit invasion had begun to include our fenced in yard. There would often be one or two adult rabbits at dusk or dawn, sitting on the grass. Our front yard gave them a sense of protection from any dangers in the neighborhood—people with their dogs on the sidewalk going past, the memory of that bobcat—our little plot of land welcomed them and we let them feel at home. When I set our dog out, she would give a creaky run as they slipped through the white picket fence. Once she came back inside, smiling and out of breath, the rabbits would return to settle for the night.

Then one afternoon my wife called me at work and said, "I have some bad news."

"What is it?" I answered. "Tell me quick."

I don't need the suspense.

It turned out our dog discovered a rabbit nest. Nest? I didn't even know they had nests. I thought they lived safe in tunnels underground. What are they doing building nests like birds? She explained on the phone and I could picture it. Soft grass, the fur pulled from their mother and padded like a little cloud, then covered over in a blanket of fitted green on the lawn. The grass is tall around the base of the little red leaf Japanese maple tree. I whir around it with the push-mower until it has formed a miniature jungle island. That's where five baby rabbits had been left to grow.

Our old dog with her misty eyes and crooked leg found them there and rooted them out and carried one, cupped in her mouth, to the front door.

I'm sorry if it seems a golden retriever has become the villain in this story—it's true when

I got home I had a hard time looking at her—I know she was only following her nature, something planted deep in her mind. She didn't realize she was doing wrong. She finally caught her rabbits. It didn't matter that they were helpless and young. The one in her mouth squeaked like a toy.

My wife and daughter put three of them back in the nest, but kept two. One had a broken leg and another one was bleeding. Those two, they wrapped in a blanket and Coral kept them covered on her lap. My wife called to tell me they were on the way to the animal rescue clinic and I could picture where that was.

Outside of town, off the Mount Baker Highway, beside a bend in the Nooksack River, cold green water rushes below the old rusted arch of the railway bridge. We haven't been there in years. We used to take Coral and she would make pies out of mud and dig her toes in the shallows. Our dog would wade out in that fast jade current until she came out far downstream. She would get out spindly, sleek as a seal, and shake the water off like a painting left on the dry smooth rocks.

The clinic was peaceful and cool when they brought the rabbits in and the woman said they would do what they could. I like to imagine the rabbits came through fine. They were set free out by that big wave of blackberry and later on in the twilight they will tell their story to their starry-eyed young, fresh from the nest. I know that's what Coral wanted to believe. That would have been a good ending, but something with a gothic tale to spin had drawn us in.

The next day it rained.

The temperature dropped. Looking out the window, I spotted a puff of brown beside the maple. Our toy binoculars revealed the bunny in the grass. That's when we really invited this lesson in, when my wife carried the frail drop of life into our home. I found a small cardboard box that we lined with cloth and we dried the tiny creature off and set it by the heater and played Mozart and Bach. For Coral, who always wanted a rabbit, this was a dream come true. She's been asking me for a pet rabbit since she was three. Thanks Beatrix Potter, thanks Richard Scarry. Her wish came true when they went out to the nest and brought that sad animal in.

I do believe you have to look after the world around you, not just your family—your family goes past the walls of your house. I'm sure we saved it from a cold water death; I'm certain we showed it a world where it was safe and we cared for it as best we could.

Coral fed it lettuce which it nibbled up. It watched us with bright eyes and tumbled about and peered over the cardboard edge. But this wasn't to be one of those soft cartoons we used to watch. Some things can't be fixed like machines brought in from the rain. Living things are molded and turned out by the earth and made back into that clay again when they die. That arrangement was clear when we spotted a small white maggot squirmed in the corner of the box. Had it come in with the rabbit or did it fall out of it? Maybe it was the only one. Maybe there weren't more tucked in its flesh. There's a thought for you—barbed as a thorn. Every miraculous life comes with death built within. That isn't an easy understanding.

Once the rain was done and dusk was falling, we brought the little rabbit back to its nest. The mother would be along soon. She could have worn a watch. She would arrive around ten of nine.

Two rabbits grazed across the street. Using the binoculars, I could tell they weren't her. But while I was watching them, she slipped into our yard.

As I'm writing this, some time has passed. She is out there now, under the red maple. Her children are gone. She is listening, maybe even tuned into my thoughts. I wonder: is she willing to start all over again? There's a nice breeze tonight. The sun shines orange in her ears. Actually, I can't tell…maybe it's not her. Maybe that's the one baby that survived? They grow fast. There's a whorl in the daisies where it comes and goes. Interesting that it would still come back here, after all the tragedy. Once it's 9:30 and I've watered the plants, I leave three carrots by the tree. Nighttime has arrived… shadows and the sounds of cars when they pass.

One of the worries I had, one of the stories I heard, is if you handle a baby animal, helping one back to its nest, the mother will not take it back, that somehow the presence of a person will keep her away. The clinic told us that wasn't true. After all, what a pleasure it was to see her return to them. She nursed and groomed that tiny rabbit and I hoped she was able to heal it completely. But I was also worried about something they said at the clinic about how fragile these new babies are. Their skin is like tissue paper. Their bones are like rubber bands. Still, you had to hope everything would be okay.

The next day was sunny.

We checked the nest and there were three rabbits, but one was dead. This wasn't supposed to happen. The two surviving rabbits hid along the fence. With binoculars I could recognize the one we brought inside; it was smaller. I also couldn't help notice the fly that followed it. A big blue bottle rested on a leaf next to it. I was afraid to mention what I saw. The ears would twitch and it would hop, but the fly would follow. I could see it like the dot of a warplane, or a drone just biding its time. I knew its presence was death.

It would be nice to think they had more of a chance. But if they did, we would really be run-over with rabbits. They'd be like barnacles. I'd have to go outside every morning and scrape them off the lawn and the driveway just to make a path. Out of the five, only one lived. To see it return to us, we greet it like a sailor back from the sea.

Not everyone does. I've heard people with gardens curse the roaming deer and rabbits.

They feel forced to take precautions. The other day I saw our neighbor mowing the lawn with a pistol on his belt. Once I saw a wire trap set up next to his house. Is he like the villain in *Chitty Chitty Bang Bang* who put children in cages? It looked like a crab trap but who knows; maybe he traps and shoots rabbits? My wife says I'm letting my imagination go.

After years, Joe's Garden down the street from us surrounded their lush crop with a mile of electric fence. People curtain their flowers and hide their ornamental trees behind cocoons.

Not Dilly though. His plot of land beside his house is open to anyone. Sometimes in the morning I'll see a deer in there, watching me pass on my way to work. "I try to grow things they don't like," Dilly told me. Only the tomatoes are kept safe, in a hand-built greenhouse that ripples plastic sheets like sails. Somehow after all these years the animals and Dilly have come to an agreement. I don't know what it is. I don't know how it works. Maybe he talks to them.

When you can look into their eyes, you know that's not impossible.

Communication doesn't need to be written

down or transmitted through radios to be understood. I won't forget that last evening when the mother rabbit came back to our yard. The two babies had been waiting for her. As usual, I was watching them with binoculars. (I hope those binoculars weren't getting me a reputation with the people going by: joggers, strollers, dog walkers. I was like a lighthouse in the window).

Seeing the mother rabbit's arrival, they threw themselves across the grass. Through the glass, they broadcast their happiness. The little one tumbled in a hurry to her side. That's the moment in life I'm so glad that baby rabbit got, that feeling of joy. It's no different than anything we've seen in a movie, at an airport, or after a long time away from the one you love. That tiny rabbit's life was no more than what you could cup in your hand, but it got to have that gift.

Sometime in the night, that little one died. My wife found it outside of the nest, on the grass, and we buried it in our backyard. Coral spoke to the flower left on top the ground.

She took it pretty hard. When we went back inside, Coral sat on the couch and cried. "It was my fault! I told you we should have brought them all to the clinic! You wouldn't listen to me!" She sobbed and covered her eyes. "I told you." It's hard to think about when you think about things deeply. There must be something wrong with a world where lives are so short and there are those who don't care. But this is the planet we're born to. It isn't an easy world. People especially should know better, to lead by example. Maybe it will spread?

It would seem our dog hasn't learned anything from this misadventure. She still takes to the yard with her ears cocked and looking. When we went to Lopez Island last weekend, there were rabbits everywhere. I overheard someone say she never saw this many on their island before. The people on this island though are used to being overrun. The ferry comes five times a day, unloading tourists and campers like us. Especially in the summer, it's an endless migration. No wonder. You should see the beautiful blue water, the rocky islands that surround the view, osprey, eagles, whales and seals, farms and rolling yellow fields. Ever since I first visited this place, I always wanted to live here. If I didn't have to worry about money and a job—I guess if I was a rabbit!—this is where

I would be. And the rabbits love it here too. They must have subways taking them all over the island. They live next to driveways, under porches, in grassy parking lots; they order coffee at cafés and room service from the Islander Hotel. I saw one on a tractor seat. I saw them at a yard sale. When I took our dog to the Farmer's Market on Saturday, we sat beneath a shady apple tree. The rabbits had gnawed all the lawn short as a crewcut and left signs of their digestion scattered like buckshot. I leaned with my notebook against the bench when we were greeted by a large rabbit. It left the bramble like a saloon door swinging. It was a lot bigger than the ones on 32nd Street back home. If it had boxing gloves, I think our dog might have met her match. Madison Square Garden would have been packed that night, dense with carrot cigarette smoke and jeers as our old dog in the corner stepped out at the sound of the bell. Maybe then she would have learned her lesson. She craned her neck under the apple leaves as the undefeated rabbitweight champion sauntered to another sunny patch of flattened grass.

I wonder what the Ohio rabbits will be like. A long time ago when we lived there, we shared some moments together. I used to take Coral on walks to Bunnytown. It was only a short way from our rented house. The road turned a corner, and folded out next to the buckeyes and tall wild grasses a Frankenstein power station was built, surrounded by chain-link fence. You could feel the hum and snap in the air. Around it was gravel and mowed lawn. We could always count on a few rabbits being there. The sight of them would quiet Coral and she would point and whisper. I also remember the very early mornings pushing the baby carriage at 2 AM… long pink streaks of the sodium street lamps, houses dark and huddled, the big trees hushing leaves overhead, the plastic stroller wheels crackling on the cement. The only other one awake to see us would be a rabbit. I would catch its silhouette near the park. Sooner or later, after a few blocks of walking, the lullaby of dawn would work and Coral would fall back asleep. Even as that was happening, I knew it was like a dream. Later on, like now, after twenty years have gone by, I could go to the video store and rent a copy of *Ohio Morning*.

There's a moment in that movie, *Night of the Hunter* when Lillian Gish watches an owl pounce on a young rabbit. "It's a hard world for the little things," she says. Though by the end, she stirs the pot and knows, "They abide and they endure."

It was Coral's idea to watch that movie again. She was right too; it was the perfect balm that evening. We followed those two orphans on the run as they drifted through a dream-world. It was a miracle they survived, guided as they were by currents and protective shadows, a step ahead of death. They were also quick and smart. We thought of that one rabbit who stayed alive. I don't think kindness goes unnoticed. Just look how that rabbit came back to our yard.

After the movie, I looked out the window. It was dark out there. Everything became a shadow in the sea-like pour of night. I expected to see a man on a horse, on the corner across the street. They shot him, they caught him, and a mob hunted and surrounded him with sticks and fire. But he is the sort that always returns. We must stay aware.

As I climbed the stairs to our bedroom, I wondered what Coral would dream.

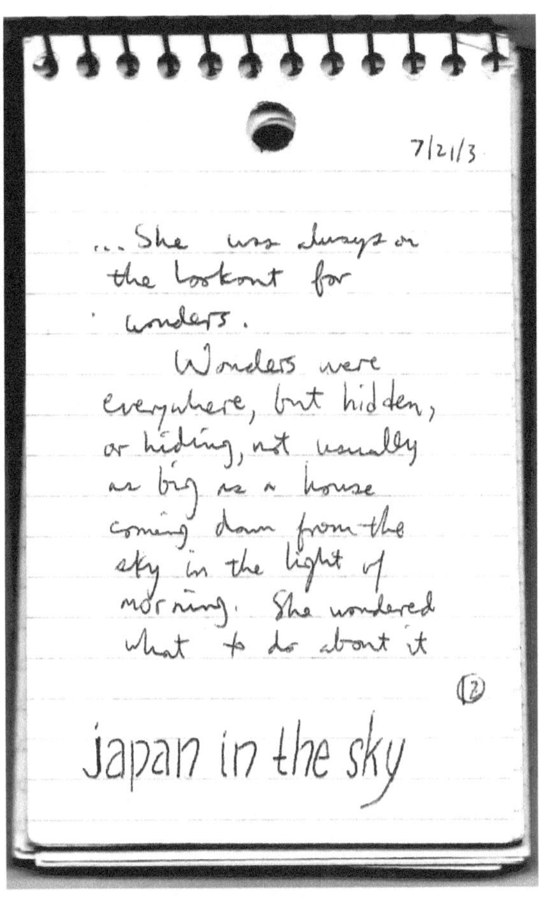

PART 2

CORAL & THE ADMIRAL

On a morning that was gray and cold, the sight of something small and square hung in the sky. It could have been a kite being pulled toward the ground. Reeled down, it came slow and carefully. The clouds seemed to hold it back and clawed around its edges.

The sound on that early morning was a breeze, a soft radio static that wished it had tree leaves to pour through. Every wind likes that sound. It was summer but you would never know. There was very little green showing. The earth almost seemed like the moon, all grown over with charcoal craters and dark shadows, even in the day.

Up there, the thing in the sky was still coming down. The flat kite look of it had changed. It was something with edges, corners, walls, glittering windows, a roof, a chimney letting a steady puff of blue smoke riddle out.

The house floated quietly through the black and white air, over the rubble and the ghost of what used to be a neighborhood.

"Tinhorn was here."

Zelda Fitzgerald said, "Don't worry."

The water splashed around her. She was a mermaid in a bathtub. She repeated, "Don't worry, dear. It's happened before. We'll catch him again." Her long finned tail stirred. "I hope he left a river for me, a creek at least. A lake would be nice. Do you see any water down there?"

"No, it's all a wasteland. There's a lot of smoke though. If there's water, I can't see it." The Admiral steered the big wooden wheel, watching out the window. "Anyway, we'll soon find out. We're coming in for a landing now. Hold on tight, my love."

The house landed like an elevator ride between pieces of torn pavement, wood, bricks, pipes and carriages.

You might think that Tinhorn, whoever he was, had caused a war and killed everything in sight, turning to ashes even the mermaid's precious water, but it wasn't so.

As the house settled into a skirt of dust, there was someone watching them. In fact, she had been watching the house ever since it started to descend. She was always on the lookout for wonders.

Wonders were everywhere, but hidden, or hiding, not usually as big as a house coming down from the sky in the light of morning. She wondered what to do about it, while she watched from a hole dug in the earth.

A salmon made a dried leaves rustle next to her, poking its nose out into the air.

"Careful," she whispered, "We don't know what that is…"

The landed house was still and quiet.

It was the first complete house she had seen in a while. Since the war began. That seemed like a long time ago. There stopped being calendars and clocks. Now she was here, dug into the basement of what used to be her home, the slanted earth veined with tree roots. But she wasn't alone, she had her animal companions. She had found them in their survival disguises. The salmon dressed in leaves, a pair of black stones in the dirt was a deer waiting to be pulled up by the horns. A shadow was a crow. A stump was a bear. There were all there with her. They lived together in the foundation of wrecked construction in their own imaginary world she called UMPTH.

"Look!" the girl whispered. "The door is opening." Her eyes and the leaf, stone, shadow and wood all watched too.

First the Admiral creaked a look outside. His great long moustache flowed out and led him through the door. His eyes were sad at what he saw.

"We've got a lot of work to do," he muttered. "This looks worse than last time."

"It'll be okay," came the gentle fishy voice behind him. The mermaid pulled herself into the doorway, the bathtub on wheels, the walls wired with strings to guide her along. She looked past him and caught her breath at the sight. "We'll have to start all over again." She touched his blue sleeve before he could leave. "I'll get my wagon and meet you."

The Admiral walked out into the day. He set a ramp from the porch to the earth. Dry ground made little clouds around his feet when he walked.

"They need rain!" he called back over his shoulder. "Do they ever…"

With the sound of squeaky wheels, the mermaid rolled down the ramp on her red wagon. This was her mode of outdoor transportation, a child's wagon. Her tail draped over the edge, scales sparkling, all green and blue and yellow.

The dazzle caught the girl by surprise. "Oh!" she cried, "A mermaid!"

The rabbit clutched her with little paws. "Don't let her eat me!" he whimpered.

The Admiral had gone back indoors, leaving

the mermaid.

Her emerald eyes scanned this way and that, looking for water especially, but the pipes had broken underground and maybe it was gone, but not for good. Some water dripped from her, off her cupped hand and made dark prints on the sand.

The Admiral came back out pushing an aerial before him, a long metal pole with coppery antennas spreading off like antlers. He huffed and puffed as he carried it and planted it like a tall flagpole into the dirt.

He turned it, dug it deep enough to root itself, until it could stand by its own power. "Ahah!" he smiled and went back into the house.

The mermaid remained there in her wagon of water. She seemed to be listening in to something hidden.

When the Admiral returned again with a roll of wire, Zelda told him, "We're in luck, not everything is gone."

"Of course not!" the Admiral agreed, as he fit the wires into the aerial. "And soon we'll have this place returning to itself." He began to unroll the wires back into the house, pulling and untangling, trying to keep them running straight. "Are you coming back inside, my dear?"

"No…I think I'll wait here and see what happens." She was peaceful and content as any Buddha.

"Did you hear that?" Rabbit whispered, terrified. "She wants to find me and eat me!"

"Don't be silly," the girl replied. "And please be quiet. I want to see what happens too."

What they couldn't see was the Admiral inside the house, bringing all that black wire to a wooden-looking potter's wheel. It was colored dusty brown with the clay from long use over and over in days gone by. The Admiral fed the silver tipped ends of the wires into two spots in the base of the wheel. "Yes," he said to himself, as he pressed the switch.

The machine coughed. It coughed again, coming to life. Then it began to hum. A faint orange light came from cracks inside. "Yes," he said again, delighted.

Along the wall were records, one after the other. He took the first one off. He would begin to play them, one by one, until their songs brought back this little part of the world.

The record he chose was a bright red. He put it flat on the potter's wheel and immediately it began to spin. What a beautiful blur it made going round and round. The old man clapped his hands together. There was no ordinary sound that a record would make, but he knew what signal was sending from the antenna out into the air. He followed the wires back outside to watch the change. Soon, a gray dead-looking land would spring with life again.

And the girl in the ground with her animal friends saw another new wonder happening. The pole pointed at the sky was doing something.

The air around it shimmered. It was like water when you drop a pebble on a pond.

"I can't look!" the rabbit cried and covered his eyes with his ears.

Sleeping further back in the shadows, the bear stirred for the first time and his nose took a deep breath.

"Oh look!" the girl pointed. Rabbit let one ear slide.

The sky, which had been a gray float of nothing for so long, was moving, slowly whirling way up above.

The rabbit trembled, "I can't watch," and curled up in a ball.

But the girl stared at the sight unfolding.

The salmon rustled next to her.

The smell of rain.

The rabbit, the bear in his dream, the salmon, the crow and the girl, all of them underground breathed in the cool fresh breeze they had not felt since whenever that was.

The sky was changing. New clouds were being drawn towards the Admiral's beacon. The clouds followed a shepherd cloud bigger than the rest and wearing painted edges. Led across sky, they gathered, went around and spun.

The Admiral hurried back indoors and chose a new record to play. He quickly took the first one off the potter's wheel turntable and put on a blue record. When it began to spin, he went outside to catch the results.

A silver sound marked the beginning of the rain. It hushed in the air. It moved in like a dream or the memory of an animal.

The mermaid thrashed onto her back and held her arms up, palms to the rain that started to fall. She and the old man were laughing. The water made dots on his navy coat.

The salmon shook, but the girl kept him from going out. "Not yet," she told him.

The rain grew to a fury. The Admiral suddenly opened a yellow umbrella and stood under its roof, but the mermaid bathed in it.

The ground was so dry the water sat on top an inch thick, waiting for the earth to breathe.

And then the rain stopped.

"Ah!" the Admiral bleated. "The end of the record." He admired the results and said, "If Tinhorn ever came to a place like this, where the people were on to him, hah! He'd fall down in the mud!" With thick steps on the slick and puddled earth, he went back to the house.

While he was gone, the water dripped from eaves, making the sounds of little bells. The pools and puddles were at work finding each other and forming a creek. Underground, who knew what water was doing? Feeding roots and seeds?

A bird could be heard. The mermaid's eyes slowly opened.

A rainbow shined, sliding from the sky and landing on the rubble place where the little girl hid.

Following the glowing colors, fifty feet from her, in the wet pool where a house once stood, Zelda had a surprise. A girl's face watched her. She had a rainbow on her but didn't know it.

"Well, hello!" the mermaid called. "I had a good feeling you were here somewhere."

As the girl came out of the ground, the mermaid and the old man were waiting for her. The mermaid offered a pale green wet hand to help her up.

"Thank you," she piped and told them, "My name is Coral. I live here."

"Yes," the Admiral said. "My name is The Admiral and this is Zelda. We're the Flying Fitzgeralds!" he crowed.

"You're a mermaid," Coral said. "You're rare."

"Yes I am," she laughed. "So are you."

Coral said, "I've seen fairies before and a unicorn one time."

"You're very lucky." Zelda smiled.

"I decided I must have fallen under a wicked spell, but I'm not afraid. I'm a sensible girl, I'm seven years old. I have magic of my own and games I like to play to pass the time."

Zelda asked her, "Are you alone?"

"No. I have my animals. They've been taking care of me."

The Admiral had brass binoculars held up in the air before his eyes. "I don't see anyone."

"They're still hiding."

The mermaid water sloshed as she moved. "Please tell them it's alright. We came here to help you."

Coral took a few steps towards them. She looked at her feet in the puddles. She walked on clouds, the pooled reflections of the sky. She said, "You made it rain, didn't you?"

The Admiral said, "Yes. That's just the start though. Wouldn't you like to see some trees and blueberries again? And wouldn't your animals like to have meadows and hear birds singing again?" The old man swung his arms in all directions. "I remember when it was all like that."

"I know what I'm waiting for," said the mermaid, "streams and rivers and lakes and the sea."

Coral told everyone, "I have a friend who is a salmon. He can't wait to be free."

The Admiral promised, "It won't be much longer. I'm directing the weather with that aerial there. I've been working on this machine for years. We wanted to start with a neighborhood first. Begin small. Then, before you know it we'll have the world back again."

Coral said, "Can I help?"

"Of course! I was hoping you would want to. See, you probably know better than me what your animals want. Come along, we can all go inside and start right away." The Admiral put his hands on the mermaid's wagon and pushed all her water forward, towards the house.

"Do you want to bring your friends?" Zelda asked the girl.

"Well, maybe I'll bring Rabbit. He gets scared very easily."

Coral pattered across the mud while they went to the house.

"We'll be in there!" called the mermaid over her shoulder.

"Okay!" Coral peeked in the still, dark entrance of her home. There were some pretty stones to kneel on. "Hello?"

Salmon rustled, kicked the stones as he nosed out a bit. The smell of rain's return made it shine and want to swim.

Coral pet the eager fish and said, "Yes, you'll have your river and I bet some lakes too. I met the people who are doing this. They're nice. I'm going to go inside their house and help them do the magic."

The bear was still asleep. The deer cast a shadow with the shapes of the others pushed back along the walls. Coral laughed when she saw her rabbit. His ears were standing up behind a brick wall. "I figure you better come with me, Rabbit. I don't want you to be scared."

"Oh, thank you." His bright eyes were riveted to her. "I thought you must have been eaten. I thought you disappeared."

"Oh, Rabbit! Come here!"

With a bound, the rabbit leaped up into Coral's arms and she caught him and told everyone else, "I'll be back for the rest of you too. Everything is alright."

Coral carried Rabbit, a funny-shaped knot of wood, over the wet, waking up world. She heard him whimper and tucked him deeper in her sweater.

The door of the house was open. There was warm light inside and the mermaid called her in.

It wasn't like any room Coral had ever seen… a big lighthouse lantern beside the window, an old ship's steering wheel, a record rainbow that curved on the back wall, and in the middle of the room, the Admiral was busy turning dials on a strange glowing machine.

"Welcome, Coral," he said.

"Hi." She was a little shy going over to where he was.

"I need your help, Coral, to change the world. Come take a look at this."

The machine was a polished tree stump. It

grew out of the floor, stopping not quite as tall as her. The top was level and a round blue vinyl disc sat on it. The silver playing arm had lifted off, having played the record through, and it rested on a peg.

"This is what made it rain," the Admiral said. He took the blue record off and held it. "Would you like to choose what comes next?"

"Yes," Coral replied quickly. It seemed so long since she had been with people.

Hiding in the pocket of Coral's sweater, Rabbit jumped when Coral saw the wall the Admiral led her to. She couldn't help an, "Oh!"

He chuckled as he returned the blue record where it belonged. It seemed to melt into a rainbow.

"What color would you like to see on the land, Coral?"

She thought of the gray color outside and instantly told him, "Green!"

He agreed, "Good idea. Now which shade of green, I wonder? Would you like to choose one?"

The rainbow glowed and stretched from red to violet in front of her. "I like this color green," she said. She pointed at a lily pad shade.

"Oh yes," the old man beamed. He could

see dandelions, tulips, bluebells, ferns and the tips of budding oak trees. He set it on the turntable and let it play. "Look out the window, Coral. Tell me what you see."

She stood by the glass and laughed. Wherever that rain had poured, seeds were sprouting. Some of them became like Jack and the Beanstalk, trees that quickly grew taller than telephone poles. And whatever had been dry cracked ground became soft grasses, bushes and flowers.

"Look at that!" said the mermaid. She put a hand to the porthole.

"Oh, look at everything!" Coral cried.

"This is how it used to be," Zelda told her.

"What happened?"

"Tinhorn." The Admiral's voice was cold. "He wants it all for himself. He doesn't want to share. And you can see what he's done to the world to get it."

"Why doesn't he see what he's done?"

"He doesn't live out here with us. He has a palace. He thinks everything is fine his way."

A breeze made all the new leaves whisper. You could hear it through the screen door.

"Can I go outside?" Coral asked.

"Of course!"

The house stood in the middle of a garden and Coral hopped off the porch into it. While she jumped around like a kangaroo, the Admiral set his hand on the mermaid's smooth shoulder. They watched the butterflies surrounding Coral. Birds appeared on the aerial branches, finches, a cardinal, a mourning dove. A forgotten broadcast band had tuned them in. He said, "Just wait until we get more than that antenna to broadcast with."

Coral lifted the salmon outside and placed it in the shallows. With a splash, he was off and gone, following the current's flow. The deer emerged, followed by the crow and a sleepy looking bear. Coral brushed the crumpled leaves off his back as he ambled past. Her animal friends were just as pleased as her to find this patch of land.

When Coral returned to the porch, she gave Zelda a red flower.

"Thank you. What a treasure!"

"It's a flower," Coral told her. "Do you have these in the sea?"

"We have our own kinds of flowers. We also have mountains, deserts, forests, meadows with bees. You would love it there."

Coral thought about riding a sea turtle,

flying it to places like this, underwater. She was going to ask if the fish sing like the birds, when she caught sight of something in the sky. "Is that another house?"

The Admiral stepped around her and took a look with his binoculars. "Oh no…"

"What is it?" Coral asked, "Another house?" It didn't look that way.

"Is it raining houses?" Rabbit worried from her pocket.

"He knows we're here!"

"Come here!" Zelda held out her hands to Coral.

"Who is it?" Coral hurried into the house.

The Admiral quickly followed them. Already the light in the windows was turning to night. "Not friendly," was all he had time to say.

The screen door blew aside and a horrible shape blundered in, flapping bat wings, shrieking, hot wind blowing everything to smithereens like the howling Big Bad Wolf. Coral was thrown from Zelda's side as the thing burst around the room.

The Admiral shouted, "We need light!" but Coral couldn't move. She held to the floorboards. She didn't know where the mermaid was, it was like being in a roaring tornado. Everything was breaking and crashing around her.

He wasn't a real Admiral, but he knew how to reach through the dark terror of what was happening and he turned on the lighthouse lantern. They only used it in the foggiest weather, or on Tinhorn's shadows. The bright blast filled the house and the shadow gave a yell, then all that black whirlwind flung itself out the door.

"He's gone," the Admiral said. With his hand over his eyes, he turned the lighthouse lantern off. "Oh no…" he sighed. A bomb could have gone off in the room.

Coral opened her eyes. It looked like the house had been turned upside down and shaken. But worst of all, the mermaid's bathtub was tipped over. The water was all gone; it was empty as a shell. "Where did Zelda go?"

The Admiral crunched across the floor. He glanced at the red wagon tossed against the wall, the rainbow of records, broken and askew, and he stopped with a hand on the empty bathtub.

"Did she disappear?"

"No, she's still here." The Admiral bent over and carefully picked up something small as a feather.

His old palm trembled, held opened flat.

The mermaid had shrunk and turned into cellophane. It reminded Coral of the Fortune Telling Fish she got at Fuji's Five & Dime. The little red papery fish would twist and wiggle when you held it on your hand. The envelope it came in had written predictions and the fish would tell your fortune depending on how it moved. Coral didn't want to get too close, afraid her breathing might blow the mermaid away.

"She will be alright," The Admiral said. "This happens when she runs out of water." He put that delicate shape in a china cup. "We'll keep her safe until there's ocean again. Don't worry, Coral. It won't be long." He saw the worry on the girl's face and he patted her shoulder. "We're going to get her that water."

"Where?"

"We can be there tomorrow morning. We're going to Tinhorn."

That scary shadowy shape that spun and roared? Coral bit her lip and told him, "Let's chop him in half!"

"No, it doesn't make sense to kill him. He will just come back and do the same thing. He needs to learn. We have to show him how his plans won't work. The world will be better off when he learns."

"How?"

"We get past his shadows. We bring back the rain." The Admiral chuckled, "Sounds simple, right?" He looked around the room. "But first we'll have to get this house shipshape again." He passed her Zelda's cup and said, "See if you can find somewhere safe for her, Coral."

Coral held both hands around the smooth china. The mermaid outlined in the snowy white cup spoke in a faint voice to the girl. "We didn't get much time together, did we?"

Coral shook her head. She was afraid how loud she would sound if she answered.

"Don't worry, Coral. I'll be fine. I can wait in here for things to get better."

Coral nodded. She saw a good place for the cup and she helped the Admiral sweep and straighten. She was sure they would be okay.

It seemed okay until the Admiral held out the broken halves of a cloud colored record. "This is the record I use to make us fly. And it's broken now." He set the pieces on the turntable.

"Can we glue them?"

"Nooo…" he sighed. "I'm afraid not."

Coral hadn't been this close to the turntable before. It was amazing that a tree could play all those songs. They could even lift a house.

"What are you thinking?" the Admiral asked her. She was so serious.

"These words…" She kneeled and ran her fingers over the carved letters in the bark. "Pottery, Pottery, Pottery." It was repeated in a thin line that went all around.

"That's the maker's stamp. Originally this was used for pottery."

"Pottery, pottery, pottery," Coral continued and then her finger stopped on, "Poetry."

The Admiral took a look, "Yes, you're right."

"Does that mean that poetry works too?"

"I don't know. I can't make pottery or poetry. I just use it for playing records."

"What if I make a poem about flying?" she asked. She hopped to her feet. "I know how to write poems."

"You do?"

She nodded and described it for him, "First you run straight, then you look behind you and you find something that's moving and you look in that spot for words. Write them down in your notebook. You keep doing it until you have your poem."

The old man's eyes widened. "Yes, that sounds worth a try."

"I need to go outside though."

The Admiral stood beside the lighthouse glass, just in case another shadow appeared, and he watched out the window. Coral certainly looked like she knew how to find the words, running around on the lawn, collecting poetry. She had an amazing way, she would run with her notebook, or leave it on the grass to come back to. When something moved near her feet—a branch, flower, leaf, a ladybug or the blue dragonflies—she would stop and it would tell her what to write. She ran, stopped, turned and she searched, getting low to the ground. She pounced, dug quickly into the grass, the stalks of dandelion, then she laughed, got up, turned around, and ran back to her notebook and finished the words. She waved at the Admiral in the window. "I found it!" she called and hurried inside.

They cleared the turntable for the page from her notebook.

"Does it have a name?" he asked.

"I want to reach up and pull the sky down."

"That's good," he nodded.

"Maybe all we have to do is make it turn,"

Coral said, "like a record."

"Let's try."

"Where there's a will, there's a way," she said.

As soon as she pressed the switch, as soon as the machine purred and the slip of paper began to move around, the house lifted from the ground.

Coral clapped her hands. "I knew it!" She ran to the window. They had left that green corral like a windblown scrap and were up in the clouds.

Taking hold of the wooden ship's wheel, the Admiral announced, "Next stop, Tinhorn!"

Coral got thoughtful and her smile slipped away. "Who is Tinhorn anyway?"

"He's the one who keeps reappearing, trapping and tricking, getting his way. Oh, he's done this before. He's predictable in his ruthlessness. Everything he does is destructive."

"But what is he?" She remembered that shadowy tantrum that attacked them and she glanced nervously around the room.

The Admiral caught that scared look and shook his head. "That wasn't him that came here, that was just a shadow. He uses them to make mischief."

"He's a bull with one tin horn," Coral

decided.

The Admiral had to laugh, "Don't let him think he's any more than that. Tinhorn gets his power by making people afraid—fear! He can't do anything if we don't want to be afraid. He's the one we need to learn to grow beyond."

They could take precautions though, to make sure his shadows didn't revisit them. They lit candles on the windowsills and the Admiral tromped up the stairs with the lighthouse lantern. He brought it up to the top floor tower of the house and let it shine round and round. By that time it was nighttime. The moon followed along with them. It looked like Coral could reach out and touch it.

She made a bed for herself in the bathtub, blankets around her, and the sound of the sea cupped in that curve. "Early to bed, early to rise," she yawned. All she needed now was a story to put her to sleep. She decided she would like to hear about the water, the ocean, water so wide you couldn't see the other side.

The Admiral creaked in his rocking chair and began, "I'm not actually an official Admiral. Years ago, long before we met, I began my journey to you with a suitcase."

"Is that when you saw the mermaid?" she

asked.

"No, that came later."

"Where did you meet her?"

"I'll get to that."

"Was she in a lake?"

"No."

"A river?"

"No, Coral."

"A swimming pool?"

"Actually, it was the moon. But first, I was flying over the sea when I saw a sinking ship below." He held his hand high above the other, then let it drift down. "Of course I swept down to see if I could help." A flying house hovered beside a tilted steamship. The blue ocean sparkled. "I leaned from the porch and shouted out—hello?"

The ship was deserted except for one man in the wheelhouse. He opened the door to the flying bridge and his lonely voice drifted up, "This is the Admiral…"

The old man told Coral, "I wasn't the Admiral yet. I was just someone in a flying house. So I asked him if I could help. Was there crew I could save, would he come aboard? He wouldn't do it. He said everyone else was gone, but he would go down with the ship."

"Why?" Coral yawned.

"That's what they do. They take the responsibility if something has gone wrong. I couldn't change his mind to leave that ship, but he wanted me to take his suitcase. He tossed it across to me."

"What was in it?"

"Only this uniform that I'm wearing now." He tapped the gold braided sleeve.

"That's how you became The Admiral."

"That's right."

Coral yawned again. "Then how did you meet the mermaid on the moon?"

He grinned, "I bet you've always wanted to go to the moon too?"

Coral shut her eyes, "Umm…no."

"What! Really? Well, I saw Zelda in my telescope one night. She sat right on the tip of the crescent moon, like a girl on a swing."

"Why was she on the moon," mumbled Coral.

"Why not? It's just another place. And it's not so far if you have a flying house. We were meant to be together."

That's what Coral wanted to hear. With that thought, she fell asleep.

The Admiral made sure they were safe as

they drifted through the clouds. The candles on the windowsills, the lighthouse lamp sweeping, the hum of her poem, kept them from harm. And in time, the sky began to lighten.

Coral woke up when the house bumped to the ground.

She sat up. The window was silver as a nickel coin. Melted candles lined the sill. She said, "Are we there?"

"Close enough," the Admiral spoke from the other side of the room. He shut his suitcase and said, "We'll go the rest of the way on foot."

Coral wasn't long getting ready. She couldn't tell, looking out the window, what they were walking into.

"Okay," said the Admiral. He carried the suitcase, but he used his free hand to point at her, "Hey, you've got your shoes on the wrong feet."

"No I don't."

"Did you put your feet on backwards then?"

"No." Coral didn't mind that her shoes were on the wrong feet. They felt better that way. She stamped on the floor to show him.

"Okay…it's a bit of a walk though."

"No time like the present," she said.

He laughed. He couldn't help it. Where

does a seven year old pick up those sayings? So many things were placed along the way and as they grew, they held onto what they liked. The Admiral remembered songs he'd love to hear again for the first time. Wouldn't it be fun to learn the world all over again? He opened the screen door and out they went.

They were back on gray, ashy earth.

"It looks like where we started," Coral said. Her bright blue sweater made her move like a tropical fish.

The Admiral stopped at a half buried car and set his suitcase onto its roof. "Before we go any further, we have some disguises to wear." He opened the latches and revealed a suitcase full of soot. That's what it looked like, but as he pulled out a layer, it unrolled like a coal cloud. "Tinhorn's not the only one who can use shadows. These are sheep shadows. They're soft, they wouldn't hurt anyone. Here, put it on."

"What does it do?"

"He won't be able to see us in these shadows." The Admiral took out the other coat and put it on. Now he looked like an arctic explorer. He left the empty suitcase where it was. They could get it when they returned. He was sure this would work. "We can do this together,

Coral."

"I know." The shadow covered her like a warm blanket. She held the edges to keep it around her as they left sight of the house.

It wasn't long before they came to a fence. Blackberry vines pressed and leaned against it. The way through it was a gate, guarded by a dog. The dog held a book.

Coral whispered, "Is that dog reading a poem?"

"No, it's a joke book. He's the Door Dog. He's waiting for us."

"We have to get past him?"

The Admiral nodded.

The Door Dog heard them and shut the book on his paw and stared their way. "Who goes there?"

"Me," Coral told it. She guessed it was a knock-knock joke and she was right.

The dog asked, "Me who?"

"Me, that's who!" Coral shouted.

"Okay, okay, okay," the Door Dog winced and held the gate open for them. He riffled the pages trying to find her answer in his book.

Coral gave the Admiral a quick glance, but he was staring ahead at their next destination. She could see it too, a gold palace in the distance, surrounded by a shadow moat.

He spoke when they were clear of the wall. "I have to warn you, before we go any further. There's a lot of confusion around Tinhorn."

"Like that guard dog?"

"Right. There will be more like him before we get to the palace."

"What if there are monsters?" Rabbit worried from her pocket. "What if they tell us, 'We eat rabbits!'" and he growled fiercely to prove his point. Suddenly his eyes widened, "Who was that? Who growled?"

"You did," Coral scolded him, "Just be still."

A coyote made from dust and wind heard them and ran away.

A clown in a rowboat sat in a sandbox, fishing.

They walked across a dead field full of sleeping bees.

"Shhh!" the Admiral whispered.

The field became a place full of parked cars, all facing a drive-in movie screen. A pole with a speaker was posted in the ground beside every empty car.

Stopping next to one, the Admiral couldn't resist—he turned the speaker dial and listened. He didn't know if he was listening to a long forgotten movie soundtrack, or was it just the radio?

A voice crackled from the static. "This is the Admiral…" against the sound of a polar wind, "This is the Admiral…" It echoed just the way it sounded so long ago from the deck of his sinking ship.

When Coral listened to the speaker next to her, she told him, "I can hear crickets at night, on the other side of the world."

Beyond that enclosure, mourning doves on slumping wires over where flowers used to be. Coral followed the Admiral. A little bird didn't like the sound of them trespassing in that ghost of a parking lot. "Can you be any quieter? It's only because you're so much bigger you get to do what you do! Nobody listens to you when you're small." Then the sparrow grew to a person's size and ran across the twigs and dust. It got smaller again in the distance.

While this was happening, Tinhorn's palace was shimmering over the barren land. It was shaped like an upside down pyramid, with the point stuck in the earth.

"Pssst!" someone called from behind a telephone pole.

Coral pulled the Admiral's sleeve and

pointed.

Someone in a shadow that wasn't a sheep's leaned towards them. "Come here a minute," he beckoned.

"Do you have something to tell us?" the Admiral asked.

"What do you need?" He reached into a shadow pocket and held out a vial. "20 drops of water." His eyes widened at them.

"Why don't you pour that on the ground?" The Admiral told him.

"Wait! Where you going?" He put the vial back in his shadow.

"We're going to Tinhorn," said Coral, "and you can't stop us."

"I won't! I won't. Listen, I'm here to help. You'll never get there walking though. Look…" Like some magic trick, he pulled a mirror out of the telephone pole. "You can use this mirror to go to the palace." He turned the glass of it around until it faced Tinhorn's direction. "There's nothing to be afraid of. People have been walking through mirrors for years," he promised.

The Admiral wished he would have been holding Coral's hand. Before he knew it, she stepped forward and with another step into it, she bounced off the glass.

"Ouch!" She lay on the ground and shook her dazed head.

"It only works for his followers," the Admiral explained as he lifted the girl to her feet. "Are you okay?"

"Well, what do you know?" the man said, putting his mirror back.

"We don't need that. We can get there walking," the Admiral told him and he took Coral's hand. "We have to stay together. We're almost there." He pointed at the buzzing palace, "We're in the suburbs now."

The hard packed dirt had turned to cement. There used to be houses and yards, cars and trees with tire swings. Now it was all flattened out. A dustbowl.

While they were walking along the sidewalk, an angel fell from the sky and splat on the cement with a tar-like mark. He hopped right up and greeted them, "Good day! Salutations my friends!" He stood in their way with his hands held out, with cheap miracles up his sleeves. "Are you feeling downhearted? Do you need help making rent? A new job? Someone to care?" Anything that seemed disastrous, he was prepared to repair.

"Don't listen to him," The Admiral told Coral. "He's just another one like before. All he has are empty promises."

She nodded.

"He can't hurt you. He's just talk, talk, talk."

"I'm not scared of him," Coral said. She was more interested in getting to the end of the crumbled street. It fell into only one more stretch of gray dust before the palace. Being almost there made her hurry. More debris… empire litter, it looked like a dirt flashflood had roared across the plain.

They walked by a pile of dumped voting booths, tangled together like birdhouses. Coral saw the American flag painted on each one. As they rounded that wall, they came to a kind of beach. The ground gave way to a black rolling lake of shadows, the moat before Tinhorn's palace.

Coral sighed, "Now what do we do? How do we get across?"

"We find someone with a boat…" The Admiral said. "Look, there's one there."

He and Coral found themselves standing beside a wooden rowboat. Was it waiting for them? A handwritten note was left on the plank seat and The Admiral read it aloud, "The

Curly Q Cat is off playing with the field mice. We haven't seen him for a while."

"Do you think he would mind if we use his boat?" Coral said.

The Admiral turned the paper over. Nothing more was written on it. He shrugged. "I don't know. I guess it's okay. We'll bring it back soon." He gave it a push and the bow slid easily onto the shadow. "Are you ready?"

"We've come this far," Coral said. "Nothing ventured, nothing gained."

The Admiral laughed and steadied the boat for her. She sat in the bow while he dug the oars into the shallows and sent them from the remains of land.

"We're floating on all these strange shadows," she said.

"As long as they don't notice us," he said, "we should be fine."

She said bravely, "I'm not worried."

In Coral's pocket, under the layer of cloudy sheep, Rabbit stirred, speaking in a muffled, crumpled voice, "I'm worried. I always worry. I need to. If I worry about things, they won't come true. If I don't worry about them, then they might happen."

"Oh, Rabbit," she whispered and patted her

pocket.

Shadows climbed over each other, swept and washed around the bright gold palace like a thick black lake. Above them, circling gulls, burnt as cinders, followed them without flapping their wings.

She listened to the crackling waves, the rhythmic oars, the sighs of shadows.

The Admiral paused, pulled an oar into the boat so he could reach beneath his cloak, and he said, "Here, take a look through these." He passed her his binoculars.

Instead of shadows, Coral could see rows of lemon trees growing. What? She brought the glasses down then looked through them again. More magic? The meadowy world returned. What a difference, to see all those green leaves with lemons. But the shadows were back as soon as she left the binoculars. She didn't know what to say.

"Without them it looks so cold and dead, doesn't it?" He started rowing again. "This is the despair he's projecting. The real world is underneath his spell. Now look at the palace."

Instead of the gold, Coral saw it for what it was. A cement bunker built into the side of a hill. Tall, shimmering antenna towers grew from it like thistles. "All that glitters is not gold."

The Admiral said, "It's a shame he fooled so many people. But it won't be for long."

Without the binoculars, she watched Tinhorn's palace. It didn't glow quite the same way. Now it didn't remind her so much of an upturned pyramid, as something she had seen in an antique store—back in a dusty corner, a curiosity—a Victrola windup record player fitted with a cone-shaped flower of brass to project music. Tinhorn's palace was nothing more than that. A few more yards of shadows, and she would find out.

The bow rode up over a splash of blackberry and nightshade shadows as they crunched ashore in front of the palace. Coral hopped out and held the rowboat while The Admiral followed.

"So far, so good," Coral said. She wasn't fooled by the gold anymore; she knew something else really stood there.

The Admiral opened the door. He didn't need the binoculars to know, it was just a cement hallway. Fluorescent lights flickered above, buzzing like mosquitoes. Ahead of them was another door. "That's the place," he said.

He reached back and took Coral's hand and they went into the radio studio.

Tinhorn was on the air. His voice rung like a sour bell, but he was nowhere in sight. The room wasn't that big—where was he? The walls were lined with records, more than in The Admiral's flying house, and ahead of them was a sound board, with tapes stacked up and a microphone bent down to a chair. That's where Tinhorn spouted those simple-minded words. He needed his voice amplified, sent out by tall radio towers across the land, otherwise he was too small to be heard. He was no bigger than a locust, waving his arms and ranting on the chair.

The Admiral moved quickly. He had a jar in his hand and fast as can be, he bottled Tinhorn up like a lightning bug. He screwed the lid on tight. That was it.

Quiet.

Sometimes you forget the sound that isn't there, that hides in between all the things we do. Catching it can be harder than capturing Tinhorn. Coral closed her eyes and floated in the calm.

The next sound she heard was The Admiral cuing up a record, the gentle settle of the needle on vinyl and the whirr. A snapping like a campfire in the speakers, then the song began. It was the song of a blue record, the sound of rain.

The Admiral said, "Will you come outside with me?"

"Sure!"

The open doorway at the end of the hall was lit silvery blue as a fish. The hush of pouring rain out there swam in the hall and tickled the skin.

The Admiral took the china cup out of his pocket and showed Coral.

"It's Zelda!"

He nodded, offered Coral the cup and asked, "Do you want to bring her back?"

There'll be bluebirds over
The white cliffs of Dover,
Tomorrow, just you wait and see.
There'll be love and laughter
And peace ever after,
Tomorrow, when the world is free.

PART 3:

CRYSTAL BEACH
Good as per Agreement

PICNIC TICKET
CRYSTAL BEACH
Good as per Agreement

PICNIC TICKET
CRYSTAL BEACH
Good as per Agreement

PICNIC TICKET
CRYSTAL BEACH
Good as per Agreement

PICNIC TICKET
CRYSTAL BEACH
Good as per Agreement

PICNIC TICKET
CRYSTAL BEACH
Good as per Agreement

PICNIC TICKET
CRYSTAL BEACH
Good as per Agreement

PICNIC TICKET

11 OHIO DAYS

1.

Lights of the city leaving. Farmland at dawn. A windmill. The Platters on the car radio, headlights on the highway. That's the spot where a coyote was earlier, in the dark grassy median.

Clocks have spun us into a new time zone. The lack of sleep, the long hours inside an airplane's metal tube full of noise and baby distress, that freezing air, then finally walking wobbly through the airport…these are the impression of planetary travel. I don't want to remember the discomfort of the flight. Now it seems like something else; now we're safely here it seems like a fairy tale. Did we arrive by butterfly? A big yellow swallowtail landed dusting the ground, dropping us off by flowers. We stepped off the wings and it was warm in Ohio, even at 5 AM. Even in the dark before the sun began. Soon we can catch some sleep in the room upstairs.

No sound of constant interstate cars, the loud airplane and cold cramping of that chair. We are here.

The birds and the trains, calm comes down, the hot of the day rising, filling the air. I don't know where the story of the day will go, but I let go.

I don't even want to think about him or say his name, but he comes up in conversation and hesitantly, just a mention, nobody really wants to talk about him. There is such a horrible feeling invoking him, whether you support him or not I bet—he always leads to anger. Quick, change the subject, look around you.

Ride a bike to the lake. Petals fit patterned into the streets.

Yes he finds his way into conversations, but it was getting easy to forget about him with other things going on—listen—the cardinals and mourning doves and The Fleetwoods' harmonies left on the kitchen windowsill while we go back to the beach to looks for missing glasses. Alyssa is 9 and she left them somewhere on the sand when she went swimming. It becomes *The Case of the Misplaced Spectacles* and we carry rakes and buckets and I ride a bicycle to lend a hand. You don't know what you'll find on the shore of Lake Erie when you're dragging the sand. The air is hot as an open oven, a buzzard coasting overhead, wings held out wide and black as a flying monkey from Oz. We made a commotion, searching the shore. Some people we didn't know joined in. The little stones winked in the shallows. If she wore her glasses into the water, it would take a submarine to find them. It looked futile, so I walked across the roasting sand, looking for the stranded remains of those black frames reaching out of the dunes, until I got back on the bicycle and rode home. I figured with a nine year old, there's a pretty good chance she left them somewhere inside the house. I thought that would be the sort of thing a seasoned television detective like Columbo would know. But everyone showed up a few minutes later in the car and Alyssa had her glasses on. It turned out a family not twenty feet away from the excavation had them the whole time. "Oh, we found some glasses," they finally admitted, holding them out as if they weren't aware we were searching, and that's how the investigation ended.

I'm seeing the Ohio wildlife again after a few years away. A cicada made of green and blue stain-glass rests on the road beside a parked car tire. Later on, after spaghetti, I spotted our first Ohio rabbit chewing grass in the next door neighbor's yard. Ears held out like television antennas—the old kind, connected to the top of your set that you need to turn to get a better signal from the air. Sometimes a crumpled ball of tinfoil helps. Not much different from the rabbits in our yard, this one is probably tuned in to the same TV show we know.

When I was riding a stiff blue bicycle from
the lake, the starlings all took off and the wood-
chuck in the field waddled to the edge of the
creek and listened to me whistle. He recognized
the song. I know he knew it, before he hid back
in the ground.

It's a different sort of acceptance here. I guess
because they know so many people, friends and
coworkers and neighbors who voted for him.

She asked me to guess how old she was and
I said 12. Kids like it when you think they're
older. She told me she is 9, but she has a friend
who is 10—and she held a hand well below her
shoulder—who is only this tall!

I took my sandals off to walk to the water's edge, but the sand is burning hot and I quickly put my shoes back on. When I get back to cement, I can wash my feet cool under the street faucet.

It's hypnotizing—the big white well-kept houses, lush green lawns with the sprinkler going and the blasting heat of the day.

Back at work, my boss and I would get so upset looking at the news. We felt part of what was going on, but helpless, like the tar baby sitting at the crossroad, melting anything that touches its black goo.

At the bird feeder, birds flash back and forth. Hear an unseen dove on a wire.

Making wooden whirligigs, getting orders from neighbors, relatives and the town dentist wants one too.

Pied Piper is at its best late at night, when you see that ice cream cone sign lit on the roof. People arrive like moths. A 1932 convertible looks like a man driving a bathtub. It's warm as pool water when you get out of your car. The crickets are going mad in back the parking lot along the railroad tracks. Cones, Crunch, Dip, Waffle, Quart. Sundaes, Shakes, Malts, Floats. Juicy Freeze. Strawberry Shortcake, Brownie, Frozen Banana only $1.25.

Our son sighs at the end of the day, "Isn't it strange that we got to Ohio today, even though it feels like we left home a million hours ago." The ceiling fan whips the air overhead.

2.

He demands attention: on the TV, the radios, newspapers, the casual talk in wicker chairs…until a mourning dove, or a train will interrupt.

Like those endless words flowing into a paper cup, I keep thinking we need The Beatles to arrive and play the Blue Meanies away. People need a better song to follow, don't they?

He has no real power if people would stand up to him and not be afraid. The Emperor has no clothes. All those fairy tales and fables are true. It's biblical, it's epic, old as campfire stories; everything big will fall…He will become nothing, not even a Roman emperor; there will be no statues to him.

Cardinals, cicadas, doves cooing, with the garbage truck wheezing and braking by the curbs. Rattle of glass and hydraulic lift. The dragon finally fades away, replaced by the usual sounds of the day.

The week before we arrived, he was already here, bringing a rally to Ohio. Back during the election, his plane also flew to our town. A comic book billionaire with his very own jet. It could be seen over our islands and bay. He needs his fill of yells in his ear. He can't live without the constant attention. Could he sit on a porch in a rocking chair and be quiet with his thoughts, until everything craven crawled out and scuttled for a rock to hide under?

It's painful and awful to think of him, to dial him in. I can sit here, let him come and go, listen to the birds, hear the dull roar of a distant mower, the rise and steady fall of the cicadas.

"Triggers the flight-response in deer. Odorless to humans. Safe for vegetable gardens. Air flows through the station, carrying repellant scent across your garden. Trusted for generations! Money back guarantee.* Keep out of reach of children. Penetrates deep into the soil where animals burrow. This unique blend of ingredients causes a mild irritation to animal's nasal passages. When an animal touches, tastes or smells, it triggers the natural instinct to escape/avoid and the animal simply leaves. People and Pet Safe when used as directed."

A red newspaper machine stands outside the restaurant door. He's in the headlines, telling us what to believe, as if he creates reality. I don't want to think about him.

By the way, where is the circus lady? I've been promised an introduction. Every morning she's supposed to be at the beach, but she's always somewhere else.

Presenting Mrs. Nettie Jump
& The Blue Blowers

A small town main street, a few blocks from the lake, in an old wooden building filled with fans and printing presses. They kept every working part of the newspaper's history, from the typewriters, the drawers filled with Gaudi font letter blocks, and rolls of brown paper ready for the stories to flow. The walls are covered with posters, signs and announcements. In a stack of crisp newspaper copies, I find *The Erie Echo* from Thursday, June 14, 1961. "Mrs. Nettie Jump Dies; Ninety Years of Age. One of Vermilion's elder citizens passed away Sunday afternoon following an illness of one month." Next to a sign in heavy lettering—"No Politicians on Premises"—is a poster for a dance that happened long, long ago.

The Great
BLUE BLOWERS
White Hot Music
Just What the Doctor Ordered
A Youthful Organization
of Syncopating Melodeous
College Tunesmiths
Appearing At
CRYSTAL GARDEN
Grand Winter
Opening Sun. Dec. 19th
Admission—Gents 50¢ Ladies 25¢
Free Dancing All Evening
Dancing Every Sunday Evening
and Holidays

The Great
BLUE BLOWERS

White Hot Music

Just What the Doctor Ordered

A Youthful Organization of Syncopating Melodeous College Tunesmiths

APPEARING AT

CRYSTAL GARDEN

GRAND WINTER

OPENING

SUN. DEC. 19TH

ADMISSION—Gents 50c   Ladies 25c
FREE DANCING ALL EVENING
Dancing Every Sunday Evening
and Holidays

There's a woman in Oberlin with 54 typewriters.

Providing The Area's Finest Drinking Water

A mile bike ride on the side of Cleveland Road, past the neighborhoods and over the Huron River. The birds fly up from under the trestle, where they rent their nests at summer rates. The Great Lake clouds pile thick and tall; overstuffed with warm sweet-smelling rain. There was a little that fell on our windshield coming home, but these clouds are waiting, you can tell, like cows headed in from the field.

When I got to Riverview Lanes, I rode around the side into the parking lot reserved for Bowling Alley Customers Only. I stopped beside the dumpster, leaving the bike there, knowing it would be safe. (I found this to be true all over town: at the IGA, the library, the Goodwill, the drugstore, the beach, the visitor center, the cemetery.) But when I tried the door, it was locked. The neon beer sign in the window was on. It's a big building. There are two more doors on the other side but I found each one locked. Nobody goes bowling on a Monday afternoon. It was something I had to learn by trying…the hard way, in 90 degrees… riding a bicycle through parking lots, past sailboats for sale, over a bridge held aloft by the wings of nesting sparrows and mud swallows, and my shadow was hot enough to jump off into my reflection.

Back at the house I went right to the kitchen for the gallon jug of White House drinking water: "Artesian Springs. Since 1957." This morning when I was carrying it at the IGA, the manager asked me if I needed help finding anything else. I already had the water but I was also looking for ice tea. They didn't have the kind I wanted. "Last time I was here, there were half gallon sizes," I said, "but that was three years ago. I guess you weren't expecting me."

Libraries are open doors to odd people, all people really, but certain odd types definitely. That's where I met D a long time ago when I worked the circulation desk. Every day he would stop by to bend my ear. His favorite topic in those early days was the water on Mars. D was convinced it was there and I already agreed from years of reading Ray Bradbury. But after the election was stolen in 2000 and we slid into invasions and endless war, catastrophe was all D could talk about. It physically affected him. I watched him get old and weak and those hands that used to describe the glass Martian aqueducts shook when he spoke. Every angry day he spent reading on the library computer, he would report to me. It got worse the more the country stayed at war. I'll admit, sometimes I would find some errand that took me away from the counter, when I saw his slow approach.

That's why he caught me by surprise one day when he mentioned my daughter. He had a present for her. He reached into his coat pocket. Sometimes he saw me and Coral at the store. Whenever it happened, we would wave hello. I'm glad he could remember the thought of her as something bright. What he wanted to give her was a gray chuff of fur glued to two plastic wheels, with a silver key on its back. It was a toy mouse. You could turn it and it would spin a circular whirr until its energy gave out. I remember how much Coral liked it. She played with it on the kitchen floor at our old house on Franklin Street.

Ohio's 12th Congressional District will hold a Special Election while we're here. In the county seat's city museum lives the tin man from the 1939 World's Fair. We'll be seeing him soon. I wonder if Elektro will get to vote.

Is it too much to ask for someone wise, someone trustworthy and caring who will lead us the way a green canoe will paddle along from the shore of a tangled pond, mindful of that fallen log, calm enough as it paddles deeper that you know tomorrow will be just as beautiful as today?

Bedtime and I opened the window so I can hear that thunder. The big clouds piling up all day have finally delivered. The windows shake with rain and the bowling alley that was closed this afternoon sounds like it's open now. All things in nature are alive.

Before it was a plaza, the Drug Mart and the IGA, before the Dairy Queen on the corner, there was a field. Way back in the tall yellow grass was a green building. What was it? What was it for? Someone must remember.

They just moved to their new house by the lake. Their daughter was 3. They decided it was the right time to buy a color TV. Back when my wife's favorite show was *Sesame Street*.

The storm is gone. The night is calm again. Crickets,

3.

"Head east on Mohawk Drive."

The $400 Gorilla

Halfway through my first cup of coffee, I heard about a man who drove to Florida to help a friend. His friend needed to move his circus collection. Afterwards, he got a deal on one of the attractions. It was a thousand miles back to Ohio, with the window open to stir its fur.

"Pat Brown was afraid of animals. When he went to visit Bill at the dairy, if a cow showed up, Pat would back well away."

"She's doing okay. She works at a Goodwill store, in the back."

You can't go the Blue Hole anymore, don't even try. The white cars will surround you before you get across the road. It makes you wonder what they're hiding. Before there were locks on the gate, the shore was littered with beer cans and people could stand beside the water and watch and wonder if it dropped all the way to China. It used to be a mystery, but now it is something more.

Another place I wanted to go in Ohio was a watermelon farm. I thought I could stand amid the rows of their green smooth backs. I would buy two and wear them as shoes. But there are five farmers sitting on the porch when we pull up. One of them answers, "No watermelon this year," and explains why, "We're too old."

It's almost funny to think of those old men trying to harvest and move such heavy fruit, and I suppose in previous years they had migrant farmers to do that for them. I didn't ask.

Only a half mile away is a new building, big as a Wall-Mart, dropped onto what used to be fertile tomato fields. Now, tomatoes are being grown inside those gray painted walls, out of the earth, no windows, no sunlight, no connection to us, like a zoo with locks on the doors. Another building holds the workers shipped here from Puerto Rico. What's going on, Ohio?

The Know-It-All Club of Ohio

Their president is a teenage boy who will talk about cars all day.

At the Family Dollar store, five girls in red t-shirt uniforms are being trained by the manager. When he claps his hands, they scatter like cardinals.

4.

Advice for a Woman in Cleveland

This very moment there's a woman in Cleveland looking out the window. She misses the islands of Washington State, Mount Rainier and its crown of snow. Starting a new married life, something always gets left behind. You have to make your heart big enough to love where you are.

Around us this picture of a dinosaur land, unseen croaks and whistles, an estuary dappled with lotus, where a heron can reach through the yellow reeds to spear a meal. In the visitor center is a magic map. Sensors on the floor mat let you go back and forth in time. First, you can see Ohio's Coastal Wetlands pre-European Settlement. Then, by simply shifting to your other foot, you can see Ohio's Coast Wetlands Circa 2000. "Ohio has lost over 90 percent of its historical wetlands area."

This weather lends itself to sitting in chairs, talking on porches, thoughts around dinner tables, beaches and benches set in parks. By all accounts, this should be the land of philosophers, open to dialogue, solving the troubles of the world.

The Vermilion Lighthouse, 1877, overlooks a parking lot, pink flowers in hanging baskets, and an ice cream shop. It's been moved from a lonely stone out in the lake to this spot. Nearby, I picked up a cicada lost in the sand and carried it to a chestnut tree.

"The yellow building at 5506 Liberty Street, owned by Clarence Wolf, is one of Harbour Town's oldest homes."

3 Rules for Teachers, 1872

1. Teachers each day will fill lamps, clean chimneys.
2. Each teacher will bring a bucket of water and a scuttle of coal for the day's session.
3. Make your pens carefully. You may whittle nibs to the individual taste of the pupils.

He would park the car and take her upstairs to the third floor where she had ballet lessons. Then he went across the street for coffee. He said he felt the eyes of everyone in the diner while he read his book for an hour.

A place along the lake, in the very space where the Cherokee ponies would stop beside the shore when they were set free to graze.

5.

There's a yard rabbit here too. It likes to rest in the unmade bed of the garden, in the fold of warm earth, listening to motors and birds, just alert enough.

"For many years, Huron residents used the Lake Shore Electric Railway to travel to neighboring towns and students relied on the trolley for school transportation."

I'm at the library, looking through some newspapers for the election results. It's air-conditioned, a vast quiet room, a few other people around. *The Columbus Dispatch, Akron Beacon, The Cleveland Plain Dealer, The Toledo Blade, The Sandusky Register.* The sound of crickets is still going in my ears. The librarian takes her first break, smokes a cigarette in the shade of Shirley Street.

"Free video rental with every child's prescription."

The shape of a buzzard floats next to me.

"Have fun in the water, but know that blue-green algae are in many Ohio lakes. Their toxins may be, too. Avoid swallowing lake water."

"Folklore states that for every sailor lost at sea, a mermaid's tear for him would turn to glass in the Lake Erie sand."

3 Clues to the Circus Lady

1. She has a blue bicycle.
2. Sometimes she parks it at the beach in the morning.
3. She lives on Franklin Street.

A man at the Liberty hangar has been making a plane for 15 years. He let me look in the skeleton. As soon as it gets covered with corrugated metal skin, with its windows and wicker chairs, and three engines purring over Lake Erie, it will be like 1929 again.

"**Hindenburg**: A hearty chicken salad plate served with in-season fresh fruits. $8.95."

It's so green around here and the warm summer rain rattles the world when it storms, but back home I know the yard has turned yellow and it's hard as bundled straw.

6.

A fly doomed to spend all day walking up the wall of window. No, not quite. I just caught it ice skating on a slice of watermelon.

On Russia Road

After the rain, a blue haze hovers above the field. The cows decided not to move. As usual, they wait for the weather to change.

I'm still thinking of the frog I saw yesterday. I was stopped on the bridge so I could look at the marsh. A chalk white egret. The dark water bubbled. A blue heron hunting further off. A fish broke the surface in the middle, safe from them. Before I started pedaling again, I saw a dead animal ahead, on the shoulder of the road. Car tires sung on the bridge going by me, near and fast. It was a dead frog. On its back, its white belly looked painted. It was big too and looked just like a toy—the kind that would squeak if I bent to press it with my toe.

This is a land where you are aware of the insects in the background, always talking night and day.

A butterfly manages to swing itself around the speeding car. I don't know how it regains its simple scribbled flight path across the road.

American flags decorate this dip in the road dedicated to a killed staff sergeant. It's only a brief view, the scene from a country bridge, trees shading a stream with fish and birds and passing cars, the same peaceful way it was before the wars.

Lake Erie Seahorses

Somewhere along this lake in the 1950s was a roadside store. It was filled with those things summer tourists love to buy. Most amazing of all, on the wall was a fish tank filled with living seahorses. It was easy for those children born in the 1940s to fill a bucket with Lake Erie water in hopes to catch a few.

We rent a small colored ball for each of us and try to knock past dinosaurs, lighthouses, ramps, pits, grates, corners and other obstacles until, with a little bit of luck, we arrive at the end of 18 holes.

7.

I dreamed I was somewhere I don't want to be. Even though I'm tired, I don't want to sleep and go back there. Maybe it's part of going to that Liberty hangar and seeing their military collection. It's hard to say exactly. I want to sleep but I don't want to go back there. Maybe it's safe, maybe the danger is gone by now. I guess I'll find out when I close my eyes.

When the mourning doves take off flapping, every songbird in the yard disappears too. The feeder swings lonely as one of those railroad lanterns, as a hawk lands silently in the laurel tree.

The recruitment billboard leaned in a farmer's field reads, "The Fighting Spirit of an Entire Nation" and our way of life drives by in milkweed, purple chicory, a blur of grass, fast food, car lots, pawn shops, pharmacies, houses nailed together, the church on the corner with the red traffic light.

A cloud cut in half, clean as a bread knife slice, set like a loaf to cool in the blue sky.

Columbo in Ohio

The evidence? A cigar smoked down to an inch and left on the side of the road.

"**Ohio In The Ice Age**: This picture shows Ohio at the time of the Mastodon, during a lull in the ice sheet movement. The time period is approximately 12,000 years ago."

"**Johnny Appleseed**: This apple tree was planted by Johnny Appleseed in Richland County, between 1812-1815."

There was a different future in store. There would have been robots like Elektro in every house if it wasn't for the war. That's when his wife was melted down for her aluminum. His dog Sparko was scrapped in 1972. Elektro's head was removed from his body and forgotten in a basement for 50 years. He hasn't had a cigarette since 1956. But Elektro's been put back together. Things are better now. At least we think so.

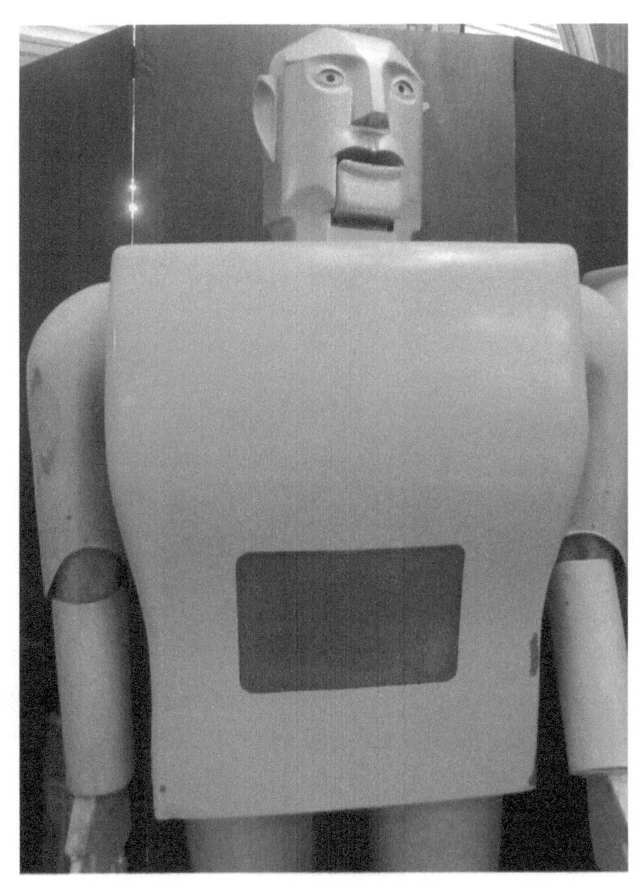

8.

Main Street passes a prison with two rows of razor ribbon wire. When you are freed, you get a pair of clothes and ten dollars bus fare. The grain silos are tall as the abandoned buildings. We see two Confederate flags on the way to sirens downtown.

A jukebox with a song you didn't count on.

Don't worry. All the warplanes are pinned behind glass. They have been made small and harmless, as out of reach as those bats that peep and scratch the air overhead while daylight falls.

Doreen has a trapdoor that takes her to the roof. At 4 AM, she goes up there, long hair trilling with electricity and she stands in the rumble of lake thunder, holding it tight to her like a crumpled paper bag filled with flashes of lightning bugs.

He pushed her long hair out of her eyes. You can tell he loves her even though she looks so much like her mother. Seeing her isn't easy. They won't even shop at the IGA where she works, where she rings up prices and there's always a moment of silence, fingers rubbing over the receipt she tore.

From this height, looking out the window, I can see the sparrows have made themselves at home in the chimney. They are having a garage sale up there, selling sunflower seeds and down.

A machine is made to catch all the time spent waiting around and it weaves miraculous long bolts of cloth from the minutes lost.

Queen of the Lakes, Mobile Homes

A big lawn with an empty playground. The first drops of rain.

9.

Right away we run into trouble with reincarnation. I'm drawn to a silver ghostly-looking car parked by itself, set up on bricks, tireless, in a weedy lot. I know that I've known this car before, that if I get in I will remember driving at night along the moonlit wall of tall corn splashed by the fan of headlights and the roar of a Pontiac V-8.

"Then he sent out a dove from him, to see if the water was abated from the face of the land; but the dove found no resting place for the sole of her foot, so she returned to him."

No wonder Jesus was so familiar. We've seen him before. When the show is over and we're back in the car, Coral tells us the story. Around the time the Crystal Garden was shutting down, the wax museum sold their collection to the highest bidder. The highest bidder was a church. They assembled a mighty wooden building, big as an ark, and filled it with air conditioning and wax figures. Yes, suddenly it became clear what it is about those faces: we've seen them in the movies. They were given sloppy wigs and someone had sewn them into satin robes. Paul Neman led a paper maché camel. Rita Hayworth in a shroud was caught in the stagelighting. We saw all the stars: Bette Davis, Walter Pigeon, Elizabeth Taylor, Humphrey Bogart, with Claude Rains as Judas.

A foreign language that can only be heard in thrift store radios, or read on the slivers of wood you find off the path, or washed up, painted over with sand.

The Rialto Theatre built in 1911 has been turned into an ice cream factory. A long line of people wait to get to the counter. Suddenly a man bursts through the crowd holding the melted hand of one who was too soft, too sweet, made too fragile to make it to his car.

Let's assume we know about butterflies. Some girl on Zenobia Road sits by her window and cuts each one out of paper. She paints their wings with her autograph, winds them up and lets them fly. She is an artist unknown to the world and she spends every moment of the day making something so beautifully, utterly absurd.

The flowerpot overflows with alligators. They hold their mouths open greedily. The sunlight dries on their teeth. Someone better water them. Carefully.

A man on crutches with one leg leaves his car and crosses the parking lot. His wife gets out and stands looking the other way.

"At one time Passenger Pigeons existed in the billions, and were known to blanket the skies of North America. The last Passenger Pigeon died in captivity in Cincinnati."

10.

The Foghorn wakes me this morning. An electric rain dove, on the end of the pier, calls out to those birds lost in the layers.

Two doves nuzzle and hop and the telephone wire sways like jump rope. I make love to a peach instead, hold that soft fuzz close to my lips and sink my mouth into that juice so sweet you catch your breath.

A bike ride visit to the cemetery in the sunny morning. Below the wide arms of the oak tree in the middle of the lawn, headstones of all sizes are sown. There doesn't seem to be any order at all and there is plenty of room for more.

John Flammond, Interpreter, War of 1812, died 1827.

Most of the words are so worn you can't read them anymore. This is a special language, affected by the weather, like the gray ripples on the lake, or sand ridges carved soft as snow. In this earth are the bones of the 3 Hansons: Arthur 1874-1877, Oscar 1883-1885, Walter 1876-1891.

Before I leave, a strip of white paper calls to me. I pick up that shroud and see it has writing on it too. I'm ready for anything now. Some message from the world beyond…

It's a delivery order receipt to a house on Buckeye Road. A Special Medium Deluxe pizza. The Promise Time is 6:43.

Imagination rules the world.

11.

Fishing poles lean against the cement ledge. A lot of people park their cars at this end of the road. The broken remains of the old bridge head a hundred feet more into the lake then stop in a heap of slanting dust and rebar. Sumac and bulrush grow. People find spots to fish. One guy stops us and warns us they aren't biting. He's been here two hours and nothing is happening. That's okay we say. We step over the rubble and I think of the cars that used to use this for a road. The ghosts of them run through us.

We find a good place next to a family from Vietnam. The men are fishing and a boy sits on a table-sized slab of concrete playing his radio. Later, when we leave, they're still here and we give them our bag of unused bait.

We got that shrimp at the Snack Shack. While the kids were picking lemonade from the cooler, I looked in the backroom. It was just what I hoped it would be. Bubbling aquarium tanks and washtubs connected by hoses. Minnows could be scooped up in nets. A mermaid looked over the rim of a barrel and smiled. We bought our shrimp frozen in a bag and drove with it put on the engine block.

The sunset is turning the sky red. Seagulls are heading for shelter. It reminds me of the Gulf of Mexico. There's a crescent moon, the planet Mars, airplanes, stars, and across the shallow bay you can see the amusement park, like oil rig shapes lit for the night.

We listen to the Vietnamese radio song. The light is going out on Ohio. The mosquitoes are biting. On the other side of us, a lantern was lit and it hissed and glowed. It showed three men fishing from chairs. We borrow pliers from them to tie our leader. Soon we have four fishing poles hooked to the bottom of the lake.

That's the time when all you can do is wait. Patience will turn into catfish. I heard about what happened when the Secretary of Education arrived in town a month ago. Everyone knows her yacht is registered to the Cayman Islands so she won't have to pay taxes. Can you believe that? Sometime during the night, her boat was untied from the pier and it crashed on the rocks. You can't help but smile. It's the sort of thing Robin Hood would do. It gives hope to us who are here.

While we are talking, a fish bent the pole.

A second pole gave a jump too, but each one reeled in with nothing left on the hook. A catfish had gone along the line of shrimp like someone at a buffet.

Coral rubs her arms and asks what time it is. Time to go home, we suppose. Nothing lasts forever. We get back in the car, drive past the police cruiser parked at the Snack Shack. My mosquito bites would last longer than that Ohio night. We are leaving, that place is gone, but it will reappear in the morning with sunshine on Lake Erie.

FABLE
written by Allen Frost
during 2018 summer

Books by Good Deed Rain

Saint Lemonade, Allen Frost, 2014. Two novels illustrated by the author in the manner of the old Big Little Books.

Playground, Allen Frost, 2014. Poems collected from seven years of chapbooks.

Roosevelt, Allen Frost, 2015. A Pacific Northwest novel set in July, 1942, when a boy and a girl search for a missing elephant. Illustrated throughout by Fred Sodt.

5 Novels, Allen Frost, 2015. Novels written over five years, featuring circus giants, clockwork animals, detectives and time travelers.

The Sylvan Moore Show, Allen Frost, 2015. A short story omnibus of 193 stories written over 30 years.

Town in a Cloud, Allen Frost, 2015. A 3 part book of poetry, written during the Bellingham rainy seasons of fall, winter, and spring.

A Flutter of Birds Passing Through Heaven: A Tribute to Robert Sund. 2016. Edited by Allen Frost and Paul Piper. The story of a legendary Ish River poet & artist.

At the Edge of America, Allen Frost, 2016. Two novels in one book blend time travel in a mythical poetic America.

Lake Erie Submarine, Allen Frost, 2016. A two week vacation in Ohio inspired these poems, illustrated by the author.

and Light, Paul Piper, 2016. Poetry written over three years. Illustrated with watercolors by Penny Piper.

The Book of Ticks, Allen Frost, 2017. A giant collection of 8 mysterious adventures featuring Phil Ticks. Illustrated throughout by Aaron Gunderson.

I Can Only Imagine, Allen Frost, 2017. Five adventures of love and heartbreak dreamed in an imaginary world. Cover & color illustrations by Annabelle Barrett.

The Orphanage of Abandoned Teenagers, Allen Frost, 2017. A fictional guide for teens and their parents. Illustrated by the author.

In the Valley of Mystic Light: An Oral History of the Skagit Valley Arts Scene, 2017. Edited by Claire Swedberg & Rita Hupy.

Different Planet, Allen Frost, 2017. Four science fiction adventures: reincarnation, robots, talking animals, outer space and clones. Cover & illustrations by Laura Vasyutynska.

Go with the Flow: A Tribute to Clyde Sanborn. 2018. Edited by Allen Frost. The life and art of a timeless river poet.

Homeless Sutra, Allen Frost, 2018. Four stories: Sylvan Moore, a flying monk, a water salesman, and a guardian rabbit.

The Lake Walker, Allen Frost 2018. A little novel set in black and white like one of those old European movies about death and life.

A Hundred Dreams Ago, Allen Frost, 2018. A winter book of poetry and prose. Illustrated by Aaron Gunderson.

Almost Animals, Allen Frost, 2018. A collection of linked stories, thinking about what makes us animals.

The Robotic Age, Allen Frost, 2018. A vaudeville magician and his robot track down ghosts. Illustrated throughout by Aaron Gunderson.

Kennedy, Allen Frost, 2018. This sequel to *Roosevelt* is a coming-of-age fable set during two weeks in 1962 in a mythical Kennedy-land. Illustrated throughout by Fred Sodt.

Fable, Allen Frost, 2018. There's something going on in this country and I can best relate it in fable: the parable of the rabbits, a bedtime story, and the diary of our trip to Ohio.